Uh-oh! It's Mama's Birthday!

Naturi Thomas

Illustrated by **Keinyo White**

Albert Whitman & Company • Morton Grove, Illinois

To my family. N.T.

Library of Congress Cataloging-in-Publication Data

Thomas, Naturi.
  Uh-oh! It's Mama's birthday! / written by Naturi Thomas;
illustrated by Keinyo White.
    p. cm.
  Summary: Jason spends his allowance buying presents for his mother's birthday,
but somehow ends up without a gift.
  ISBN 0-8075-8268-9
  [1. Mothers and sons—Fiction. 2. Birthdays—Fiction. 3. Afro-Americans—Fiction.]
I. White, Keinyo, ill. II. Title.
PZ7.T36925Uh   1997
[E]—dc20   96-10168
                                                                    CIP
                                                                     AC

The text of this book is set in Clearface.
The illustrations are rendered in acrylic on canvas.
The design is by Karen A. Yops.

Saturday is my favorite day. In the morning, I eat
pizza for breakfast and watch cartoons with Sparky.
　　And then Mama says, "Jason, get my purse, please."
I say, "Yes, ma'am!"

Mama's purse is big and heavy. It holds lipstick and keys and perfume that smells just like her. Mama takes out a brand-new dollar bill. She asks, "Jason, did you listen to your teacher all week?"

I say, "Yes, ma'am," because I did.

"Did you take care of Sparky?"

"Yes, ma'am," I answer. Sparky says, "Yip."

"Did you pick up all your toys?"

"Yes. Most of them."

"Then here you go." Mama smiles and hands me the dollar. She gets dollars from going to work all week. She always gives me the nicest one.

"Can I go out and spend it?"

"Ask your cousin Louis to come along," Mama tells me, "so he can keep an eye on you."

"Thank you, Mama!" I say. Sparky and I run out the door.

After we get Louis, we pass Mr. Ike, the mailman. "You guys have a lot of mail today, Jason," he tells me.

"Why?"

"Because it's your mama's birthday."

Mama's birthday? I didn't know it was her birthday!

I wonder what to get Mama.

Then I see a store with dresses in the window. Mama would look so pretty in the one with blue flowers. She could wear it to church. Everyone would look at her and say, "Oooh, Ms. Banks, you sure look nice!" And Mama would smile and say, "Why, thank you. Jason bought it for me." And she would give my hand a little squeeze, the way she does when I do something good.

"I want to buy this dress," I tell the lady at the counter.

"I'm sorry," the lady says, "but it costs more than one dollar."

I feel bad. "Let's go, Sparky," I say.

We go to the candy store. I remember Mama loves jelly
bears. That's what I will get her for her birthday!

The candy man gives me the candy and a quarter in
change. "Thank you," I tell him. "These are for my mama."

"She'll like them," he says.

I'm so happy I run and hop and skip all the way to the park. "Let's take a rest, Sparky," I say. We sit down on a bench.

I open the bag of jelly bears. They sure look yummy. Sparky thinks they look yummy, too.

Red jelly bears are my favorite. "Let's just have one," I tell him. Louis has some, too. Soon all the reds are gone. But that's okay—we have plenty left.

We start to walk home, but I'm still a little hungry.

"I'll eat the greens," I say. "Mama doesn't like green jelly bears anyway."

Afterwards I tell Sparky, "There's a lot of oranges and yellows. I'll eat just a few." Sparky says, "Woof!" but I don't listen.

Uh-oh! The jelly bears are all gone!

What will I do?

I see the balloon man. "Get your balloons!" he sings. "Only a quarter!"

Hey! I've still got a quarter left. I buy the biggest balloon. It's blue, like the sky.

Mama will love her balloon—I know it. I bet if we held on really tight, it would carry us up, up, up into the sky. We would fly over buildings and houses, over farms and rivers. Maybe we could go to China or Africa!

I see Willie and José. "Wow!" says Willie. "Can we play
with that balloon?"

José says, "Gimme!" and tries to grab it. Willie tries to
grab it, too. We all fall down together.

"Ouch!" I say. I rub my head.

"Hey, you guys, break it up!" Louis shouts.

Sparky says, "Woof!" and looks at the sky. I look up, too.
Mama's balloon! It goes up, up, up—without Mama and me.
José and Willie look sad. "We're sorry," they say.
"That's okay, guys. It was an accident," I tell them.
But now I don't have a birthday present for Mama.

"Let's go home, kid," Louis says, and we leave the park.

"Bye-bye, Louis," I say when we get to his apartment. Then Sparky and I walk very slowly up the stairs. My head hurts, and I feel like crying.

Some of Mama's friends are there. They've brought her a cake and presents. They say, "Hi, Jason."

But Mama says, "What's wrong?" Mama always knows when I'm sad. I don't say anything. I just go into my room.

Mama comes in after me. "What happened, Jason?" she asks.

I don't mean to, but I start to cry. "Mama," I say, "I wanted to get you a dress, but I didn't have enough money."

"That's okay, baby," she says.

"And I bought you some jelly bears, but by accident, I ate them."

Mama laughs a little. "It doesn't matter, sugar."

"And I got you a balloon, but I fell down, and it flew away from me."

"That's all right, too," Mama says.

"But now I don't have anything to give you for your birthday."

Mama puts me on her lap. "Well," she says, "today I got a cake and some nice presents, but I still haven't got what I wanted most."

"What's that?"

"A hug from you," Mama says.

So I put my arms around Mama and give her the biggest hug in the world. She gives me a hug, too, even though it's not my birthday.

"Happy birthday, Mama," I say. "Now are you happy?"

"Very happy," Mama says.

And I am, too!

Photo by Bill Thomas

NATURI THOMAS, an actress and writer, lives in suburban New Jersey with her family. This is her first children's book.

KEINYO WHITE is an honors graduate of the Rhode Island School of Design. He lives in California, where he continues to paint and to illustrate children's books.